tales on c

Cold Dark Night

celtic folktales

retold by **Linda Strachan**

illustrated by **Barbara Vagmozzi**

LONGMAN

Contents

Tales on a Cold Dark Night

One moment Andrew was watching his computer screen, about to rescue space hero Kromar from the lair of the dreaded six-legged aliens, and the next moment everything went black. Not just the game, not just his computer screen, but every light in his room had gone out, even the light on his digital alarm clock.

Andrew looked out of his window. Against the black night sky, thick, white snow glistened. It smothered all the hedges and gardens in the village and made everything smooth and even. All the street lights in the village were out, and there were no lights showing in any of the houses.

"Andrew?" his dad called up to him.

"Hey, Dad! What's happened? All the lights are out!"

His dad came into the room holding a torch. "We've had a power cut. It must be all this snow."

"Typical!" Andrew made a face. "I'd almost got to the end of the game. Now I'll have to start all over again from the beginning!"

When he went downstairs the sitting-room looked strange. It was full of flickering light from the candles his dad had put around the room. The flames from the coal fire made strange shadows on the walls.

"What are we going to do now?" Andrew moaned. "We can't even watch TV!" He slumped down in front of the fire, beside his granddad.

His granddad grinned at him. "You know, when I was a boy we used to sit around and tell stories on winter nights like this!"

"What kind of stories?" Andrew thought he was much too old for that kind of thing.

"All sorts of stories," Granddad said. "Like the one about the laird who was to be hanged the next morning, but I don't suppose you'd be interested in all that."

Andrew thought it sounded like it might be interesting after all. "Go on, Granddad," he said. "What happened to the laird?"

His granddad settled comfortably into his chair and began his tale.

One Guid Turn
(*Guid* means "Good")

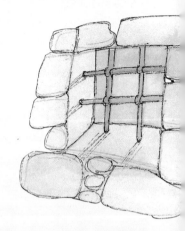

One night, hundreds of years ago, the Laird of Culzean* Castle sat in a prison cell in Flanders. It was a small, dark cell with one tiny barred window. He watched as night fell and he was very sad because he knew he would never see his home again. He was in prison because people thought he was the King's spy and nothing he said made any difference. He was to be hanged as soon as dawn broke the next day.

The Laird was sitting with his head in his hands when the door of his cell flew open without a sound. A strange light filled the small room and made the Laird look up. In the doorway was a small boy with bare feet, dressed in rags.

*Culzean: pronounced 'Cuh-lane'

The Laird stared at the boy in astonishment. He had seen him many years before. He remembered that morning as clearly as if it had been yesterday.

It had been very early on a cold winter morning when the young Laird of Culzean Castle had stopped at his front door on his way to breakfast. He had heard a loud thumping on the door. His steward was an old man and the Laird could hear him struggling to climb up the back stairs to answer the door.

Being the kind man that he was, the Laird opened the door himself so that his steward would not have to hurry. He was curious to know who was hammering at the door at this early hour.

On the steps outside was a very small boy holding a wooden bucket. The boy was dressed in thin rags and was barefoot. An icy wind was blowing down from the mountains, but the boy didn't look as though the cold bothered him at all.

The Laird, who was a tall, strong young man, shivered as he looked down at the boy.

"What brings you to knock at my door this early in the morning, laddie?" he asked.

The boy held up his small bucket. It was battered and old, but it didn't have any holes in it.

"Ma mither is mighty sick," he said, "an' I would ask ye if ye could spare some ale for her."

The Laird looked at the small boy and saw that he was scared. Something in his face touched the Laird's heart. He turned to his steward who had come up behind him.

"Take the boy to the kitchens, Hamish, and fill his bucket with ale, for his sick mother. And give him some porridge, too."

The Laird turned back to the boy. "Are ye hungry, laddie?"

The boy nodded.

"Well, go with Hamish, laddie," the Laird said and he watched as the boy trotted after the old steward, his wooden bucket held tightly in his hands.

Down in the kitchen the steward sat the boy at the table.

"I'll take up the Laird's breakfast now," he told the cook who was stirring a large black pot over the fire. "The Laird says the boy is to get some porridge."

The steward didn't think the Laird should be having beggars in his castle, but Hamish was the Laird's man and he always did what his master told him, even when he didn't approve of it.

The boy sat wide-eyed, hugging his precious bucket. He watched the cook dish up a bowl of warm porridge from the pot and put it on a tray that had been prepared for the Laird's breakfast. The steward picked up the tray and took it upstairs. The cook got another bowl, scooped a large helping of porridge into it and put it down in front of the boy.

"Eat it up now, before it gets cold," she said, kindly. He looked the same age as her own grandson and the cook was sad to see how thin the boy was. She watched him place the bucket on the table and start to eat his porridge. He tucked in and was soon scraping the last of the porridge from the bottom of the bowl.

The steward came back into the kitchen and took the boy's bucket to a large ale barrel that was standing in the corner. He checked the barrel and seeing that it was still half full of ale, he turned on the tap and started to fill the small wooden bucket.

The small bucket seemed to be taking a long time to fill, and much to the steward's surprise, it was still only half full when the ale barrel was emptied.

The steward frowned as he checked the small wooden bucket to make sure it had no cracks or holes in it, but the bucket was sound and no ale had spilled

onto the floor beneath it. He couldn't understand how the bucket was still only half full.

"I'll have to open a new barrel!" he said to the cook.

"You'd better do it then, Hamish," the cook said. "The Laird said you were to fill his bucket, didn't he?"

Hamish grunted and nodded his head. He hefted the empty barrel off its stand and opened a new one. He stared at the little bucket in amazement because it only took a few drops of ale before the bucket was full to the brim.

The boy took the bucket and, holding it close to his chest, he left the castle without saying another word.

The cook watched him go, shaking her head. "He never said a word," she said.

"Ye'll no get a grateful word from the likes o' him," the steward said with a grunt.

Now, in his prison cell, the Laird stared at the boy, and he knew that this was the same lad who had come to the castle so many years before. He looked not a day older and was still dressed in rags. The Laird realised that the boy must be one of the fairy folk.

"Why are you here, laddie?" he asked. "I have nothing for you this sorry day."

"I have come to help you," said the boy. "I remember the good deed you did many years ago. Climb onto my back and we will leave this terrible place."

The Laird smiled at the boy. "You are too small to carry me on your back, laddie. But I thank you for coming to make my last hours more pleasant."

The boy stood in front of the Laird and touched his hand. "Climb onto my back," he said, in a voice that would not take any argument. At that, the Laird

climbed onto the boy's back and the boy walked out of the door as though the Laird weighed no more than a feather. They passed the guards who didn't seem to be able to see them. The boy carried the grateful Laird to safety and, as the boy turned to leave, he said:

"One guid turn deserves another."

As Granddad finished the story, there was a knock at the door which startled them all.

"I'll get it," said Andrew.

When he opened the door a chilly wind blew huge flakes of snow into the house. There was a large dark figure standing there and, for a moment, Andrew wondered who this dark stranger was. Then he heard a familiar voice.

"Will you no be letting me in, lad?" asked old Mr MacHardy, his granddad's friend. "It's too cold a night to be standing at the door! I've just come across for a wee bit of company during the power cut."

"Come away in, Angus," said Granddad, "and get a heat at the fire. I've just been telling young Andrew some stories."

"I've come just in time then," said Angus, shaking the snow off his coat. He sat down close to the fire and warmed his hands.

"I got a real scare when I saw you," Andrew said, with

a laugh. "I wondered who the dark stranger was, standing at the door!"

"Now," said his granddad, "that reminds me of another story. One that starts on a stormy winter's night with a sharp knock at the door..."

The Seal Hunter

It was a stormy night with clouds that growled their way across the thundery sky. The seal hunter sat huddled in his cottage close to the warmth of his fire. He had no wish to go out on a night as foul as this. Little did he realise that before long he would be doing that very thing.

A sharp knock at the door took him from his warm seat at the fire. The wind nearly tore the door from its hinges when he opened it. In the howling gale he saw the dark figure of a stranger in a black-hooded cloak.

"What do you want?" shouted the seal hunter over the roaring wind.

"My master sent me to find you. He wants to speak to you on business," the stranger said. "But he insists that you come tonight, no other time will do."

The seal hunter had no idea who the stranger's master was or what business he might have with him. Still, there was something about the stranger that told the seal hunter that he ought to go with him. The seal hunter grabbed his cloak and followed the stranger out into the stormy night. The stranger led him up into the hills until they came to a high cliff. The seal hunter was beginning to wonder what he was doing out on the cliffs at this time of night. He stood shivering in the driving rain and noticed for the first time that the stranger didn't seem bothered by the weather.

"Where's your master?" the seal hunter yelled, over the sound of the wind.

"Here!" said the stranger, and with that he pushed the seal hunter over the edge of the cliff.

The seal hunter screamed as he fell. He splashed into

the water below and was pulled deep down under the sea. As he reached the sea-bed, he realised that he could breathe and see under the water!

Lying on the floor of the sea was a very old seal. The seal was grey with mottled skin and the seal hunter saw that it had a large gash along its side. The seal looked up at him with pain-filled eyes. The seal hunter looked around but there were no other seals nearby. He knew that the old seal was dying from the cut in his side. As he looked closer, the seal hunter saw his own knife was sticking out of the wound. It was red with the blood of the seal.

The seal hunter's heart ached for the old seal who just lay there looking at him. "What can I do?" he thought, "I wish I could help you."

The seal seemed to be trying to tell him something and the seal hunter drew closer to the creature and gently pulled out the knife. He put his hand on the wound and felt the flesh come together under his hand. When he took his hand away the old seal was healed.

The seal hunter was so happy that he had been able to save the seal that he vowed he would never hunt another seal again. He knew it would be difficult for him to find another trade because he had been a seal hunter all his life, but even if it meant that he would go hungry, he never wanted to harm another seal.

The seal hunter swam to the surface and he found the dark stranger there, waiting for him. It was almost morning and a low mist hung in the air. The stranger helped him out of the water and handed him a dry cloak to wear.

When they got back to the seal hunter's cottage the dark stranger said not a word before he turned and walked away into the morning mists.

The seal hunter found that the fire in his cottage was still going as well as it had been when he had left the night before. He sat down close to the fire to dry himself. He wondered how he was going to feed himself now that he would no longer be a seal hunter.

As he began to feel warmer, he noticed a large old chest sitting in the corner of the room. It was sitting in a puddle of water and was covered with seaweed. The old chest looked as if it had just been dragged from the sea. The seal hunter pulled the chest closer and with the edge of his knife, he prised it open. He couldn't believe his eyes. The chest was full of gold! He had heard tales of a treasure chest that had been lost at sea many years before and now it was his… a gift from the seals.

"Do you know any stories, Mr MacHardy?" Andrew asked.

The old man thought for a moment and then he nodded. "Well, there's the one about how the MacHardys got our clan name. It was a long, long time ago."

The Second Arrow

Many, many years ago, long before Kindroughit Castle at Braemar became the ruin it is now, it was owned by a cruel Constable. He was hated by all the townsfolk. The Constable kept a wild boar and would take any cattle he wanted to feed the boar.

The widow McLeod lived quite near the castle. She lived with her only son Sandy McLeod, and they were very poor. The only animal they had was a cow that gave them milk to drink and to sell, in exchange for other things they needed.

One day the Constable saw the cow and told his men to take it to feed his wild boar. The widow's son, Sandy was away when they came and the widow could do nothing but watch as the cow was taken away and killed. She was sitting by the fire weeping when Sandy came home.

"What's the matter, Mother?" he asked, when he saw her sobbing. "What has happened?"

When his mother told him that the Constable had ordered his men to kill their cow Sandy was angry. He knew the Constable had plenty to eat, but he and his mother would starve without their cow. He took his bow and arrow and stormed out of the house.

His mother ran to the door and called after him. "What are you going to do, Sandy?" she cried.

"If the Constable has taken our cow I will take his boar." With that he set off to the castle to hunt the boar.

Sandy was a perfect shot with the bow and arrow and it wasn't long before he had shot and killed the boar.

The Constable was furious when he learned that his boar had been killed and the next day he sent his men to take Sandy prisoner. Later that day, the widow got a message that her son had been sentenced to death by the Constable. The widow felt desperate. What should she do? Without wasting another moment, she sent a message to the King to ask him to save her son.

The King was travelling nearby and, on reading the widow's message, decided to stop and find out more about what had happened. He went to see the Constable and then sent for the widow McLeod to hear her side of the story. He called for Sandy to be brought before him to hear his judgement.

"I am told that you are a perfect shot with the bow and arrow. If you can shoot a tuft of grass off your mother's head at one hundred paces, you will go free."

Sandy's mother gasped when she heard the king's words, but she had faith in her son.

The next day a large crowd came to watch the King's judgement being carried out. The widow stood with the peat on her head.

"Stand perfectly still, Mother," Sandy said.

"I will, son, I know you can do it." Sandy walked away the one hundred paces the King had ordered. His heart was beating fast. He knew he could do it, but he also knew that if he missed, the arrow would kill his mother.

He turned around and looked at her standing there. She had a proud look on her face and he knew she trusted him completely.

Sandy took two arrows out of the quiver on his back and checked that they were perfect. He licked a finger and tested the wind before drawing the first arrow in his bow. He looked along the arrow and let out a slow breath to steady his hand. He fired.

The arrow flew through the air. Everyone in the crowd held their breath as they watched it fly towards the widow. The arrow struck the tuft of grass and sent it flying off her head onto the ground behind her. A huge cheer rose from the crowd and the King called Sandy over.

"As I promised, you have your freedom," he said. "But I have one question for you. Why was it that you drew out two arrows from your quiver?"

Sandy stood tall before his King. His voice was strong and clear. "If I had killed my mother, the second arrow was for you, Sire," he said.

There was a startled hush from those who heard and, for a moment, they feared the King would order him to be put to death. Then the King nodded and with a smile, he said:

"You are a hardy one. From now on your name shall be Hardy."

"… and that was how the Hardy clan was named," finished Mr MacHardy.

Andrew's dad brought them all a hot drink and some biscuits. He sat down to join them.

"How about that one about the soldier and his pay?" he said. "That was a good one."

Granddad smiled to himself. "This was your Grandma's favourite story, Andrew," he said. "Did you know that at one time soldiers were only paid once a year? They were paid a guinea. A guinea was one pound and one shilling."

Pay Day

Donald was a soldier. He was the youngest soldier in the regiment, but that didn't bother him. He had always wanted to be a soldier. Ever since he had been old enough to walk he had marched up and down the street with a stick on his shoulder as a pretend rifle.

Now Donald stood in line waiting with the other soldiers to get his pay. He had been in the army for a whole year and he was due a year's pay. He knew his mother would be waiting by the fire in their small cottage, mending or knitting until he came home with his pay. He hadn't seen her for months, but he had sent a message to tell her that he was coming home with his first year's pay, a guinea. A whole guinea, one pound and one shilling! He had never had so much money before, not all at one time. There would be lots to celebrate tonight.

The sergeant had explained to all his men that this pay day was special. He stood in front of them and in his gruff voice that was always as loud as a shout, he had told them why.

"The King has issued a new kind of money," the sergeant said. "And you miserable lot are to be the first to get some of it!"

A murmuring swept through the ranks of men standing to attention. A single frown from the sergeant brought silence again.

"This new money is made of paper. It looks like this." He held up a flimsy sheet of paper. The wind in the courtyard caught it and the paper rustled and waved in the wind.

Donald glanced at his friend, Jimmy, who was standing beside him. They were not too sure about this paper. How could it be worth the same as a good solid coin? The sergeant was speaking again.

"This is a One Pound Note. Your pay will be this note and one shilling." He looked at the faces of the men in front of him. "Make sure you take care of this paper note because it is the same as a coin. If you lose it or damage it, you cannot come back and get another one, any more than you could get another coin. Is that understood?"

"Yes, Sir!" thundered the soldiers all together.

Donald heard his name being called.

"Donald MacKenzie."

He stepped up to the table and watched the sergeant tear the One Pound Note out of a book. The edge was ragged, but it still looked special. He took the note and the shilling from the sergeant and went to join his friends.

"Are ye coming to the ale house, Donald, to celebrate?" Jimmy asked him.

"I dunno, Jimmy. I should go home to my mother, she'll be waiting for me."

"She'll no notice if you're a bit late, Donald." Jimmy grinned and nudged him. "You've earned a drink, lad. She'll no mind you spending some o' your shilling on a wee dram of whisky."

Donald thought about it for a moment. His mother was dead against drink but she would never know if he had just one dram of whisky before he went home. So he went with Jimmy and his friends to the ale house where they all sat and drank their drams and talked about the King's new paper money.

It was late that night by the time Donald made his way home to the little cottage. He had had a lot to

drink and found that the road kept moving about as he tried to walk straight along it. For some reason he kept finding himself in the ditch that ran along the side of the road. Each time he fell into the ditch he stood up and tried to dust off his clothes, but he was very drunk and didn't make a very good job of it.

When he got to the door of the cottage he tried to keep very quiet because he didn't want to wake up his mother, but he tripped over the step and crashed into the cottage. He didn't see the bucket by the door and he kicked it over, sending it rolling with a loud tinny noise across the floor.

"Shhhhh!" Donald told it in a loud whisper. "You'll wake my ma!"

"As if I could sleep with all that racket going on!" his mother's voice came from the chair by the fire.

Donald tried to stand up straight so that she wouldn't know he had been drinking.

"You're drunk, Donald MacKenzie," she said, scowling at him. "Shame on you!"

Donald tried to shake his head but that made him feel much worse and the room started spinning. Then he remembered his pay. He dug around in his pocket for the precious piece of paper money.

"I've got my pay, Mother," he said, pulling the crumpled piece of paper from his waistcoat pocket.

"Looks like you've drunk your pay," his mother hissed.

"No, Mother, here it is." Donald staggered over and handed her the One Pound Note.

His mother had never heard of paper money. She looked at the piece of paper in disgust thinking her son was so drunk that he didn't know what he was doing. It made her very angry. Her eyes blazed.

"What am I to do now that you've drunk all your pay? Tell me that, you useless good-for-nothing..." She waved his precious note at him.

Donald made a grab for the note, but in his drunken state he missed and staggered across the room. "Mother, give me that note. You don't understand!"

"I understand fine!" She screwed up the money into a ball. "I want your coin in my hand, none o' this rubbish!"

Donald felt the panic start to rise in him. He staggered towards her, his eyes on the precious money. His mother glared at him and tightened her fist around the paper.

"To the poor house, that's where we'll be going."

With a sharp flick of her hand, his mother tossed the One Pound Note into the fire.

Donald watched the screwed-up note as it sat for a moment on the coals. The note would have bought them enough food to last for months. The flames flared up purple and orange. Then it was gone.

From that day onward Donald MacKenzie never took another drink. When he left the army he took to the road to tell others of what could happen as a result of having too much to drink.

"Do you know any stories about ghosts, Granddad?" asked Andrew. He loved ghost stories.

His granddad stroked his short, stubby, grey beard for a moment or two and then he nodded. "There was one my own granddad told me. It was the tale of the Selkirk soutar – a shoemaker. His name was Rabbie Henspeckle."

Bought and Paid For

It was still dark when Rabbie Henspeckle got up in the morning. He was a soutar, a shoemaker, and he worked very hard to make enough money to keep himself and his wife. He liked to sing as he tapped his hammer on the nails, making fine shoes for ladies and heavy boots for farmers. Now and again, he made a pair of boots that were a bit special.

This morning he had a lovely piece of fine brown leather.

"This would make a very fine pair of boots. Fit for a gentleman," Rabbie said to himself. He often talked to himself as he worked, mostly because he found that he always agreed with himself, so it caused no arguments!

He set to making as fine a pair of boots as he had ever made, with the piece of brown leather. It took him most of the week to finish them and when they were finished, he called in his wife to see them.

"Aren't they a fine pair of boots?" He showed her the boots which he had polished until they gleamed. "They are as splendid a pair of boots as you'll find anywhere, even though I say it myself," Rabbie said.

"Aye," his wife replied. "They are fine enough, Rabbie, but where will you find a gentleman with the money to buy such a fine pair of boots?" she asked him, her hands on her hips. "Fine thing that we have a pair of boots that no one will buy and nothing to eat!"

But Rabbie didn't let her common sense spoil his delight in the boots. He put them on the top shelf and set about making some plain boots for the local farmer.

The next morning, just before it grew light, a stranger came to Rabbie's shop. He was very tall and wore a large hat that covered his eyes and most of his face. He wore a tattered cloak that looked as if it had seen better days.

Rabbie thought he would want a pair of plain shoes or boots, but the stranger looked at the finely polished boots on the shelf and asked to try one on.

He stood and watched as the stranger tried on the boot. It fitted him perfectly. He rummaged about under his old cloak and pulled out a leather purse. Rabbie watched as the stranger untied the string at the top of the purse and pulled out a gold piece.

"This is for the boot," he said in a deep grumbling voice. "I'll be back tomorrow before the cock crows and I'll pay you another gold piece for the other boot."

With that the stranger thrust the purse back in a pocket beneath his cloak and swept out of the shop.

Rabbie ran through to tell his wife. She was amazed when she saw the gold coin.

"He said he would be back to buy the other boot before the cock crows tomorrow morning," Rabbie told her.

"He must be a fine gentleman to have two gold coins to spend on his boots," his wife said. "What did he look like, this gentleman?"

   As Rabbie described the stranger to his wife, he remembered how ragged the stranger's cloak had been. He remembered the mouldy smell that his clothes had and how the purse had been full of dust and beetles when he took out the gold coin. He didn't seem like a gentleman. Rabbie began to wonder if the stranger would be back for the other boot.

The next morning, well before the cock crowed, Rabbie was working at his bench when the door opened and in came the stranger. Rabbie handed him the boot and, without a word, the stranger tried it on. Again it fitted perfectly and the stranger pulled out his purse and paid Rabbie the promised gold coin. As the stranger left the shop, Rabbie decided to follow him.

He followed him through the dark streets past all the silent shops and houses until they came to the graveyard. Rabbie didn't like being in the graveyard in the dark, but he was determined to discover where the stranger was going.

The stranger walked up to an old grave. As Rabbie watched, the man jumped into the grave and disappeared.

Rabbie ran back home. As soon as it was daylight, he persuaded some of his neighbours to come to the graveyard with him. He showed them the grave that the stranger had jumped into and soon they had opened up the grave. Inside they found a body and it was wearing the new polished boots that the stranger had bought from Rabbie.

"Well," said Rabbie, with a grin, "he'll no be needing them, will he?" So he helped himself to the boots and took them back to his shop.

The very next morning Rabbie was up as usual well before dawn. His wife listened to him singing as he tapped with his hammer and she thought he was in a very good mood that morning. She knew it was because he had not only sold that fine pair of boots for two gold coins, but he now had them back on his shelf for sale again.

Rabbie's wife went on with her morning chores thinking of all the things they could buy with the two gold coins. A few moments later she heard a loud howl coming from the shop. She ran in, but Rabbie was nowhere to be seen. The door of the shop was wide open and she was sure there was a strange mouldy smell. She looked on the shelf and the fine pair of brown leather boots were nowhere to be seen.

She ran to find her neighbours and made them come with her to the graveyard. When they got there, they dug up the grave again. Inside they found the body was once more wearing the brown leather boots her husband had made. But that was not all… in its hand was Rabbie's cap.

They closed the grave, leaving the boots where they were and no one ever went near it again. As for Rabbie Henspeckle… well, no one ever saw him again.

"I think it's time for bed," Andrew's dad said, getting up from his chair.

"Can't we have one more story?" Andrew turned to his granddad. "Please, Granddad. Just one more before I go to bed."

His granddad glanced at his dad and gave a sly grin. "I know just the one. It's not very long."

"OK," said Andrew's dad. He sat down again and Granddad began to tell the tale.

The Tail End

An old woman lived all alone in her croft in the Highlands of Scotland. She was famous for her delicious girdle* scones which everyone said were the best for miles around. One day when she was making some scones, she left the first dish beside the window as she made the next batch. As soon as her back was turned, one of the scones disappeared.

The old woman noticed that a scone had gone missing and was careful to watch from the corner of her eye when she next turned away again. No sooner had she turned around, than she saw a tiny wood sprite come in the window. The little sprite was only twice the size of the scone. It hefted the scone onto its back and leapt out of the window.

The old woman was determined to catch the sprite before it could steal any more of her scones, so she

* *girdle*: an old Scottish name for a flat iron griddle plate

waited, ready to grab it. The little sprite crept back into the kitchen and snatched another scone, but as it leapt out of the window, the old woman spun around and clutched the sprite's tiny tail.

She pulled on the tail but she couldn't pull the sprite back. She tugged harder and harder, but still she couldn't drag the sprite back in through the window.

Then, gathering all her strength, she gave one mighty yank and with that, the tail snapped in two! The old woman was left holding the tail end. The sprite got away with the scone and that was the end of that.

But if the tail had been stronger... my tale would've been longer!